To: _____

From: _____

Attitude Pie Publishing
1835 NE Miami Gardens Drive #121
North Miami Beach, Florida 33179
www.AttitudePie.com

ISBN: 978-0-9846496-0-0

Library of Congress Control Number: 2011910257

Printed in the United States by
BookMasters, Inc.
30 Amberwood Parkway
Ashland, Ohio 44805
August 2011, Job #M8732

Irene dedicates this book to
the following birthdays and their people!

march 9
my love,
steve

march 20
adam

june 14
sean

december 4
josh

april 8
alison

april 4
mom

august 27
dad

cember 25
bernice

july 6
harry

february 2
peggy

may 31
carrie

march 8
our furry love
fendi

march 31
our newest
furry love
gucci

october 5
me!

Peggy has a BIGGGGGG thank you to all of you whose
birthday celebrations make her life wonderful!

A special dedication to
my loving parents and
in-laws who are
always in my heart...

march 9
my soul mate,
brian

april 21
ross

october 25
mitchell

october 10
meredith

january 19
cody
"Mr. Handsome"

december 10
bella
"The Princess"

october 5
irene

january 14
poppie maurice

may 12
grandpa hans

october 21
mema harriet

october 24
grandma edith

Hugs and Cupcakes! ♡

XOXO

Irene and Peggy

TODAY IS MY BIRTHDAY AND I HAVE NOTHING TO WEAR!

by Irene Klitzner and Peggy Adams

illustrated by
Carrie Lou Who

Today is my birthday
and I don't know what to wear.

WAIT!!!

Maybe my pink tutu and a BIGGGGGGGGG bow in my hair.

I want to look SO special.
I'm Lola, the birthday girl!
My party's at the gym today.
I'll get to twirl and twirl.

I really love my tutu.

YIKES!!!

My tutu is
TOO
small!!!

When did teeny weenie me,

Get so
VERY,
VERY
TALL?

Mommy, Mommy help me please.
Mommy, Mommy are you there?

TODAY IS MY BIRTHDAY
AND I HAVE NOTHING
TO WEAR!!!

OH NO!!!
I have a problem
and I need to solve it fast.

If I don't find something perfect soon,
my birthday will have passed!

Maybe Grandma Lily Rose
has a dress that fits me right.

Grandma, Grandma help me, please.
My pink tutu is TOO tight!

Grandma, Grandma are you there?

OH NO!!!
She fell asleep!

I will tip toe to her closet,
so she will not hear my feet...

This flowery dress is pretty.
Can I do my big girl twirls?

WHOOOAAAAAAAA..........
I think I'm falling!!!

Guess it's not for little girls.

Grandpa Jim will fix my mess.
He's so handy everywhere.

Grandpa, Grandpa help me, please!
Please find SOMETHING
you can share!

Grandpa, Grandpa are you there?

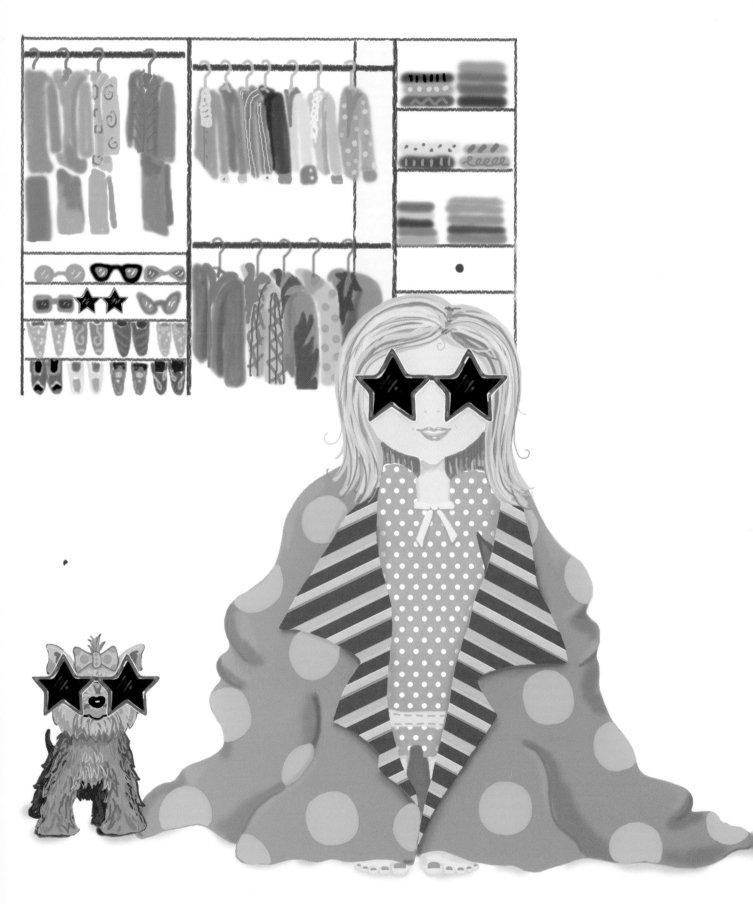

This jacket's hip and groovy.
Time to try my super spin.

WHOOOAAAAAAAA........
I think I'm falling!!!

Guess it's just for Grandpa Jim.

My sister, Chloe Joy,
will know just what to do.

Chloe, Chloe help me, please!
Can I wear YOUR pink tutu?

Chloe, Chloe are you there?

OH NO!!!
She's on the phone!
I will sneak into her closet and
find SOMETHING since I've grown...

This sparkly dress
is awesome.

Can I walk the
balance beam?

WHOOOAAAAAAAA........
I think I'm falling!!!

It should fit when I'm a teen.

My brother, Adam Josh,
is the coolest dude I know.

Adam, Adam help me please!
I'm finding NOTHING where I go!!!

Adam, Adam are you there?

OH NO!!!
He's playing ball!

I must tackle all his stuff
'cuz it's always stacked so tall...

This shirt
is totally rad.

Can I pounce
the trampoline?

WHOOOAAAAAAA........
I think I'm falling!

I don't look so good in green.

My daddy is my hero.
He always saves the day.

Daddy, Daddy, help me, please!
Make my troubles go away!

Daddy, Daddy are you there?

OH NO!!!
He is not here!

Daddy, Daddy it's my birthday
and my party's really near...

All my friends are getting ready,
with their big bows in their hair.
If I don't find something quickly...

I'll show up in
UNDERWEAR!!!

Mommy, Daddy, where've you been?

MY PINK TUTU
IS TOO SMALL!!!

Grandma,
Grandpa,
Chloe,
Adam,
don't have
ANYTHING
at all!

WAIT!!!

What's in that package in your hand?
Is it pink and frilly frills?

Did you get me what I'm thinking?
Will it give me chilly chills?

Can I do my super spin?

Can I pounce the trampoline?

Can I do my big girl twirls?

Can I walk the balance beam?

Oh my gosh, I am so happy!
My BIG bow is in my hair!

Today is my birthday and...

I HAVE SOMETHING TO WEAR!!!

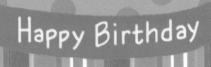

about the authors

Irene Renner Klitzner is the author of the popular children's storybook, *Sean Michael K. Whistles The Wrong Way!*, illustrated by the talented Carrie Lou Who. She is also one half of the design team for Attitude Pie Children's Clothing. Together with Peggy Adams, the other half of Attitude Pie, she has created this adorable storybook. Since her 18th birthday, Irene has been happily sharing life with her husband, Steve, in North Miami Beach, Florida. Birthdays are always a mega weekend bonanza in the Klitzner family, especially when celebrating with sons Adam, Sean, and Joshua. Joining in on the fun are her furry loves, Fendi and Gucci, her Yorkies. Sometimes, inside her closet, Irene has been heard screaming, "I HAVE NOTHING TO WEAR!!!", even on her birthday...

Discover the adventures of Sean Michael K. today!
www.SeanMichaelK.com

Peggy Hacker Adams grew up in Dallas, Pennsylvania. After graduating from Boston University with a degree in Psychology, she continued her education in sunny South Florida receiving her MBA from the University of Miami. Shortly after, she met her wonderful husband, Brian. Residing in North Miami Beach, Florida, they have raised 3 amazing children, Ross, Mitchell, and Meredith, plus their fabulous dogs, Bella and Cody. Peggy and Irene have been friends for over 20 years. Attitude Pie has taken them on many exciting adventures, but writing their first book together has been the icing on the cake!

Visit Peggy and Irene @ www.AttitudePie.com or on Facebook

about the illustrator

Carrie Lou Who is the proud mom of adorable daughter, Lola, who was her inspiration for the character illustrations of Lola in this fun and humorous storybook, *Today Is My Birthday And I Have NOTHING To Wear!*. Always an art enthusiast, she has a BFA from Milwaukee Institute of Art & Design. This is her fifth children's book and second with Irene. In her spare time, Carrie is a designer of unique jewelry and accessories, and creates original cut-paper designs. She celebrates life and birthdays in Milwaukee, Wisconsin, with husband, Rich, and daughter, Lola. Working with Irene and Peggy has become Carrie's favorite hobby!